This book belongs to:

Football Fright

By Gail Herman
Illustrated by Duendes del Sur

ADVANCE PUBLISHERS

SCOOBY-DOO!

READ & SOLVE

Find These Fun Activities Inside!

Check the inside back cover for fun things to do!

Bonus story-related activity strips throughout the 15 volumes.

Create your own mystery book, *Scooby-Doo The Swamp Witch!* Color, collect, and staple the coloring pages at the end of the first 12 books in the Scooby-Doo Read & Solve mystery series.

ADVANCE PUBLISHERS

www.advancepublishers.com
Produced by Judy O Productions, Inc.
Designed by SunDried Penguin Design
All rights reserved.
Printed in China

The gang was riding around the parking lot at Coolsville High School. It was the day of the big football game. The parking lot was packed.

TERRYTOWN TIGERS RULE

THE MYSTERY MACHINE

How many time does Daphne appear in this book?

Fred, Velma, and Daphne looked for a parking space.
Zzzzz.
In the back seat, Shaggy and Scooby snored.

"There are no parking spaces!" Fred said.

Velma nodded. "Fans have been here for hours!" she said.

"Go! Go!" A roar swept over the van.

"And everyone's been shouting for hours," Daphne added.

Just then a loud buzzer sounded.
"The game is starting!" said Fred.
Shaggy and Scooby were suddenly wide-awake.

"We have to hurry!" Shaggy cried. He and Scooby raced out of the van. "We have to get to the snack stand!"

A few minutes later, Shaggy and Scooby stood in line.
"What do you say, good buddy," Shaggy said. "Hot dogs
with the works?"
"Rulp!" Scooby gulped.

"Yeah, I'm hungry, too," Shaggy agreed.

Scooby shook his head. He pointed to the front of the line.

"Gulp!" Shaggy stared.

A strange-looking creature stared back. Then it disappeared.

"Like, what should we do?" asked Shaggy.

"Reat!" said Scooby.

"Right," Shaggy agreed. "Let's eat."

Chomp! Chomp! Shaggy and
Scooby tried to eat and carry their food at the same time.
    "Hey! Let's get a Coolsville High backpack!" said Shaggy.
"We can stash the grub in there!"

"Rrrrr, rrrrr, grrrrr." Strange voices filled the air.

Two more creatures stepped close to Shaggy and Scooby.

They were orange. Striped. And muttering in a crazy language.

"They're shaped like people," Shaggy whispered.
"But they can't be people."

"Raliens!" cried Scooby.

"Aliens!" cried Shaggy.

They dropped their food and ran.

They didn't get far. "Ruh-uh!" said Scooby.
He pointed to the sky.

"Zoinks!" Shaggy gasped, staring at the sky.

High above them hovered a spaceship.
An alien spaceship!

DETECT THE DIFFERENCE

Find the difference between the "alien" in this scene and the one below.

Answer: missing stripes on shoulders, stripes on side are green, cap is blue

"Quick!" Shaggy pointed across the field. "Let's find the gang."

The buddies stumbled through the stands. All at once, Scooby grabbed Shaggy. "Rore raliens!"

More aliens streamed through the aisles.

"Rrrrr, grrrr, rrrrr." The strange voices grew louder. "RRRRR, GRRRR!" And louder.

17

"The aliens are taking over!" Shaggy
cried. He and Scooby leaped onto the
football field. "Everyone! Follow us!"

18

Plop! A football dropped into Shaggy's hands. He looked to his right. More aliens were coming. Bigger, stronger ones. He looked to his left. Still more aliens!

19

Shaggy took off, straight down the center of the field.

Scooby's legs spun like wheels as he tried to keep up. Crash! Boom! Aliens fell like bowling pins.

The buddies raced to the end of
the field. They dove under the goalpost.
"Rouchdown!" shouted Scooby.

A crowd of aliens swooped down.
Shaggy shook them off. "Like, what do
you want?" he cried.
"RRRRR! GRRRR! RRRRR!"

Find two footballs on
these two pages, and
then find three more
on the following pages.

Shaggy didn't know what to do. So he tossed the football.

"Rrrrr! Grrrr!" One alien scooped it up. Then, in a flash, all the aliens raced away.

Shaggy and Scooby found the rest of the gang. "It's weird, man," Shaggy told the others. "All the aliens wanted was a football. And now they're going back to their spaceship."

"Aliens?" Velma repeated. "Spaceship?" She looked up at the sky. "That's a blimp," she told Shaggy and Scooby. "The kind you see at football games."

"Call it what you want, Velma," Shaggy told her. "But all these orange-and-black spacemen need to get home somehow!"

"Those aren't aliens." Velma shook her head. "Those are fans wearing face paint. Orange and black to look like tigers. For the Terrytown Tigers football team. And some are football players in uniform."

28

"But what about the strange noises? Rrrrr? Grrrr?" Shaggy asked.

"That's the Tigers' cheer!" said Fred.

"Their voices sound funny from shouting so much!" Daphne added.

MYSTERY MIX-UP?

Unscramble the letters to solve these word mysteries.

tafbolol

recsuter

pcpsehsia

eilan

retgi

ocosleliv

30

Shaggy's face fell. "And to think!" he moaned. "We dropped all that food when we ran away!" Just then the Coolsville coach walked over.

"Good job carrying the ball, boys," the coach told Scooby and Shaggy. "You really had those Tigers going. Do you want Coolsville jackets? "Caps? A team football?"

Scooby and Shaggy shook their heads.
"How about a team dinner?" said Shaggy.
"Scooby-Dooby Doo!" barked Scooby.

Create your own bonus book!

Step 1:
Color both sides of this storybook page.

Step 2:
With an adult's supervision, carefully cut along the dotted line.

Step 3:
Repeat steps 1 and 2 in the first 12 books of the Scooby-Doo Read & Solve mystery series.

Please turn page over for further instructions.

"Money!" cackled the witch. "It's all ours, now that we've scared those meddlers away!"
"Mrrphgorowl!" agreed the zombie.
The gang creeped up on the two creeps in the swampy woods… and Fred formed a plan.

21

Step 4:
Put all 12 cut-out pages neatly in order.

Step 5:
Staple three times on the left side of the paper stack to create the book's spine.

Step 6:
Congratulations, you have solved the mystery!

You have now created your very own Scooby-Doo storybook!

22